This book belongs to...

_____

IN

A

People

House

A Bright and Early Book

From BEGINNER BOOKS® A Division of Random House, Inc.

IN A People House

By Dr. Seuss*

*writing as
Theo. LeSieg

Illustrated by Roy McKie

SCHOLASTIC INC.

New York   Toronto   London   Auckland   Sydney
Mexico City   New Delhi   Hong Kong   Buenos Aires

Dr. Seuss's real name was Theodor Geisel. On books he wrote to be illustrated by others, he used the name LeSieg, which is Geisel spelled backward.

Published in the United States by Random House Children's Books,
a division of Random House, Inc., New York.

BRIGHT AND EARLY BOOKS and colophon and RANDOM HOUSE and colophon are
registered trademarks of Random House, Inc.

SCHOLASTIC and associated logos are trademarks and/or registered trademarks
of Scholastic Inc.

This BOOK CLUB EDITION published by Scholastic Inc.
90 Old Sherman Turnpike, Danbury, Connecticut 06816.

978-9-999-09211-1
9-999-09211-X

Printed in the U.S.A.

First Scholastic printing, September 2007

"Come inside, Mr. Bird,"
said the mouse.
"I'll show you what there is
in a People House . . .

A People House
has things like . . .

. . . chairs

things like

roller skates

and stairs.

banana

bathtub

bottles

brooms

That's what you find
in people's rooms.

cup
and
saucer

pillow

bed

These are doughnuts.

Here's
a
door.

Come along, I'll show you more.

Here's a
ceiling

here's a floor.

piano

peanuts

popcorn

pails

pencil

paper

hammer

nails

salt **and** pepper

goldfish

key

table

telephone

TV

Come on!
Come on!
There's more to see!

You'll see a
kitchen sink
in a People House,

a shoe

and a sock

and a clock

said the mouse.

bread **and** butter

window

wall

toothbrush

hairbrush

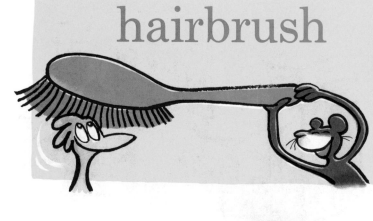

big blue ball

baked beans

bureau drawers

and

books

lights and lamps

and hats and hooks

mirror

marbles

shirt

and string

doll

and

dishes

teapot

trash

And . . .
Another thing,
it's time
you knew . . .

. . . A People House
has people, too!

"And now, Mr. Bird,
you know," said the mouse.
"You know what there is
in a People House."